Clarion Books
a Houghton Mifflin Company imprint
215 Park Avenue South, New York, NY 10003
Text and illustrations copyright © 2003 Clavis Uitgeverij Amsterdam–Hasselt

First published as *Boze Draak* in Belgium by Clavis Uitgeverij Amsterdam–Hasselt in 2003.
First American edition, 2004.

The illustrations were executed in oils.

The text was set in Akzidenz Grotesk, Cystfun, and Tannhauser.

www.houghtonmifflinbooks.com

Printed in Italy.

Full cataloging information is available from the Library of Congress.

ISBN-13: 978-0-618-47430-1
ISBN-10: 0-618-47430-7
LC#: 2003027699

10 9 8 7 6 5 4 3 2 1

ANGRY
DRAGON

by Thierry Robberecht

Illustrated by Philippe Goossens

Clarion Books
New York

"The answer is *NO!*" says Mom.

That makes me SO MAD.

When I get mad,

I cross my arms tight.

I act like I don't hear anything,

and I won't say anything.

I don't even want to

feel Mom's hands

softly touching my cheeks.

Mom says I'm like a STONE.

I feel trapped inside that stone.

I just CAN'T STOP myself.

8

It's not fair!

The answer is *always* NO.

I feel the anger deep inside,

leaping up like **FLAMES**,

making me fiery red.

11

When I'm angry,

I turn into a

GIANT DRAGON

that destroys

everything in its path.

The anger BURNS,

and I can't keep it in.

I spit out

the most awful words I know.

"I HATE you!"

A dragon never stops to think.

And a dragon has no friends.

I don't like anything,

NOT my stuffed animals,

NOT my other toys.

None of the things I loved

when I was still a boy.

Mom and Dad try holding me tight

to bring back their little boy,

but a DRAGON

is big and strong and

VERY,

VERY

DANGEROUS.

Mom and Dad get angry at me.

But a dragon listens to NO ONE!

And a dragon doesn't understand

people language anyway.

Finally, I'm left ALONE

Sitting on my fat dragon bottom

in the ruins of my room.

I feel ashamed of myself

and sad.

And then I start to CRY.

I cry so hard that it puts out

the FIRE inside me.

Mom and Dad give me a big hug.

Now I can feel

their hands on my cheeks,

and I can hear

their soothing words.

The DRAGON has disappeared,

and I'm back to being a boy.

Mom and Dad are happy that I'm myself again.

"Sometimes you're a

REAL DRAGON," Dad says.

"But we *love* you anyway," says Mom.

I'm glad I'm myself again, too.

A dragon can't fit so *snugly* in their arms.

A dragon can't tell them,

"I LOVE you, too."

But I can.